HORRID HENRY

AND THE
ZOMBIE VAMPIRE

Meet HORRID HENRY
the laugh-out-loud
worldwide sensation!

....

* Over 15 million copies sold in 27 countries and counting

* # 1 chapter book series in the UK

* Francesca Simon is the only American author to ever win the Galaxy British Book Awards Children's Book of the year (past winners include J. K. Rowling, Philip Pullman, and Eoin Colfer).

"A loveable bad boy."
—People

"Horrid Henry is a fabulous antihero...**a modern comic classic**." —*Guardian*

"**Wonderfully appealing to girls and boys alike**, a precious rarity at this age." —Judith Woods, *Times*

"The best children's comic writer."
—Amanda Craig, *Times*

"**I love the Horrid Henry books by Francesca Simon**. They have lots of funny bits in. And Henry always gets into trouble!" —Mia, age 6

"My two boys love this book, and **I have actually had tears running down my face and had to stop reading because of laughing so hard**." —T. Franklin, parent

"**Fine fare for beginning readers**, this clever book should find a ready audience." —*Booklist*

"**The angle here is spot-on, and reluctant readers will especially find lots to love about this early chapter book series**. Treat young readers to a book talk or read-aloud and watch Henry go flying off the shelf." —*Bulletin of the Center for Children's Books*

"I have tried out the Horrid Henry books with groups of children as a parent, as a babysitter, and as a teacher. **Children love to either hear them read aloud or to read them themselves**." —Danielle Hall, teacher

"A flicker of recognition must pass through most teachers and parents when they read Horrid Henry. **There's a tiny bit of him in all of us**." —Nancy Astee, *Child Education*

"**As a teacher...it's great to get a series of books my class loves**. They go mad for Horrid Henry." —teacher

"**Short, easy-to-read chapters will appeal to early readers, who will laugh at Henry's exaggerated antics and relate to his rambunctious personality**." —*School Library Journal*

"AN absolutely faNtastic series aNd surely a wiNNer with all childreN. LoNg live FraNcesca SimoN aNd her brilliaNt books! More, more please!" —pareNt

"**Laugh-out-loud reading for both adults and children alike**." —parent

"**Henry's over-the-top behavior, the characters' snappy dialogue, and Ross's hyperbolic line art will engage even the most reluctant readers—there's little reason to suspect the series won't conquer these shores as well**." —*Publishers Weekly*

Horrid Henry by Francesca Simon

....

HORRID HENRY

AND THE

ZOMBIE VAMPIRE

Francesca Simon

Illustrated by Tony Ross

sourcebooks
jabberwocky

Published by Sourcebooks Jabberwocky, an imprint of Sourcebooks, Inc.
P.O. Box 4410, Naperville, Illinois 60567-4410
(630) 961-3900
Fax: (630) 961-2168
www.jabberwockykids.com

Originally published in Great Britain in 2011 by Orion Children's Books.

Library of Congress Cataloging-in-Publication data is on file with the publisher.

Source of Production: Versa Press, East Peoria, Illinois, USA
Date of Production: February 2012
Run Number: 17107

Printed and bound in the United States of America.
VP 10 9 8 7 6 5 4 3 2 1

For the amazing, inspiring, and fantastic
Josh Stamp-Simon

CONTENTS

1

HORRID HENRY WRITES A STORY

"NO!" screamed Horrid Henry. "NO!"

"Don't be horrid, Henry," said Dad.

"We'd LOVE to hear your new story, Peter," said Mom.

"I wouldn't," said Henry.

"Don't be rude, Henry," said Dad.

Horrid Henry stuck his fingers in his ears and glared.

AAAARRRRRGGGGHHHHH.

Wasn't it bad enough that he had to sit at the table in front of a disgusting plate filled with—yuck—sprouts and—blecccchh—peas instead of the fries

and pizza he had BEGGED Dad to
cook for dinner? Did he really have to
listen to Peter droning on as well?

This was torture. This was a cruel and
unusual punishment. Did any child in
the world ever suffer as much as Henry?

It was so unfair! Mom and Dad
wouldn't let him play the Killer Boy
Rats during dinner but now they
wanted to force him to listen to Peter
read his stupid story.

Peter wrote the world's worst stories.
If they weren't about fairies, they were
about kittens or butterflies or little
elves that helped humans with their
chores. His last one was all about the
stupid adventures of Peter's favorite

 plastic sheep, Fluff Puff, and
the terrible day his pink-
and-yellow nose turned blue.
The king of the sheep had

to come and wave his magic hoof to change it back...Henry shuddered just remembering. And then Henry had shouted that a woodsman who really craved a lamb chop had nabbed Fluff Puff and then Mom and Dad had sent him to his room.

Perfect Peter unfolded his piece of paper and cleared his throat.

"My story is called, *Butterfly Fairies Paint the Rainbow*," said Peter.

"AARRGGHHH!" said Henry.

3

"What a lovely title," said Mom. She glared at Henry.

"Can't wait to hear it," said Dad. "Stop playing with your food, Henry," he added, as Horrid Henry started squishing peas under his knife.

"Once upon a time there lived seven butterfly fairies. There was one for every color of the rainbow. Dance and prance, prance and dance, went the butterfly fairies every day."

Henry groaned. "That's just copying *Daffy and her Dancing Daisies*."

"I'm not copying," said Perfect Peter.

"Are too."

"Are not."

"Don't be horrid, Henry," said Mom. "Peter, that's a lovely story so far. Go on, what happens next?"

"The butterfly fairies also kept the rainbow lovely and shiny. Each fairy

polished their own color every day.
But one day the butterfly fairies looked
up at the sky. Whoopsy daisy! All the
colors had fallen off the rainbow."

"Call the police," said Horrid Henry.

"Mom, Henry keeps interrupting
me," wailed Peter.

"Stop it, Henry," said Mom.

"The fairies ran to tell their queen
what had happened," read Peter.

"'All the colors of the rainbow fell down,' cried the butterfly fairies.

"'Oh no.

"'Oh woe.

"'Boohoo. Boohoo.'"

SCRATCH! SCRAPE! Horrid Henry started grinding his knife into his plate.

"Stop that, Henry," said Dad.

"I'm just eating my dinner," said Henry. He sighed loudly. "You're always telling me to use my knife. And now I am and you tell me to stop."

Perfect Peter raised his voice. "'Don't cry, butterfly fairies,' said the Queen. 'We'll just—'"

SCRAPE!

Horrid Henry scraped louder.

"Mom!" wailed Peter. "He's trying to ruin my story."

"There's nothing to ruin," said Henry.

"Be quiet, Henry," said Dad. "I don't want to hear another word out of you."

Henry burped.

"Henry! I'm warning you!"

"I didn't *say* anything," said Henry.

"Mom! I'm just getting to the really exciting part," said Peter. "Henry's spoiling it."

"Go on, Peter, we're all listening," said Mom.

"'Don't cry, butterflies,' said the queen. 'We'll just have to pick up our magic paint pots and color it back in.'

"'Yay,' said the fairies. 'Let's get to work.'"

"Blecchhhhhhh!" said Horrid Henry, pretending to vomit and knocking a few sprouts onto the floor.

"Henry, I'm warning you…" said Mom. "Sorry, Peter."

"'I'll paint the rainbow blue,' said blue butterfly.

"'I'll paint the rainbow orange,' said orange butterfly.

"'I'll paint the rainbow green,' said green butterfly.

"I'll paint—'"

"'I'll paint the rainbow black and hang skulls on it,' said Terminator butterfly," snarled Horrid Henry.

"MOM!" wailed Peter. "Henry's interrupting me *again!*"

"Henry, this is your final warning," said Dad. "If I hear one more word out of you, no TV for a week."

"Then the fairy queen picked up the paint pots and—"

Horrid Henry yawned loudly.

"...and the butterfly fairies were so happy that they began to sing:

'Tee-hee. Tra-la.

Tra-a tra-la

We are dainty little fairies

And we play and sing all day

Maybe you can come and join us

Then we'll paint the day away

Tee-hee hee hee

Tra-la-la-la.'"

"Blah-blah, blah-blah," snarled Horrid Henry.

He hadn't thought Peter could write a worse story than *The Adventures of Fluff Puff* but he was wrong.

"That's the worst story I ever heard," said Horrid Henry.

"Henry. Be quiet," said Dad.

Horrid Henry's fingers curled around a sprout.

"What did *you* think of my story, Mom?" said Peter.

"That was the best story I ever heard," said Mom.

"Well done, Peter," said Dad.

Bong! A sprout hit Perfect Peter on the head.

"OW! Henry just threw a sprout at me," wailed Peter.

"Did not!" said Henry. "It slipped off my fork."

"That's it, Henry!" shouted Dad.

"Go to your room, Henry!" shouted Mom.

Horrid Henry leaped down from the table and began to stomp. "Look at me, I'm a butterfly fairy!"

Horrid Henry stomped upstairs to his bedroom. It was so unfair. In the olden days, when people hadn't enjoyed a play, didn't they throw tomatoes and rotten oranges at the stage? He was only being

historical. Peter was
lucky he hadn't
thrown much
worse at him.
Well,
he'd show
everyone
how it
was done.
He'd
write the
greatest story
ever. All about King Hairy the Horrible
and his wicked wife, Queen Gertrude
the Gruesome. They
would spend their
days cackling and
making evil plans.

Horrid Henry
lay down on
his bed.

He'd get writing as soon as he finished this week's *Screamin' Demon* comic.

"Margaret! Stop shouting!
Steven! Stop grunting!
William! Stop weeping!
Soraya! Stop singing!
Henry! Just stop!
Everyone. BE QUIET!" yelled Miss Battle-Axe. She mopped her brow. One day she would retire to a war zone and enjoy the peace and quiet.

Until then…she glared at her class.

"Now. I want everyone to settle down and write a story."

Horrid Henry scowled. Miss Battle-Axe always hated his stories, even Henry's brilliant one about the Troll Werewolf Mummies who hid beneath teachers' beds and snacked on their toes. She hadn't even liked his cannibal can-can story about the cannibal dance troupe who ate their way across Europe.

It was hard, heavy work writing a story. Why should he bother when his efforts met with so little reward?

What was that stupid thing Peter had read out last night? That would do. Quickly Horrid Henry scribbled down Peter's dreadful butterfly fairies story. Miss Battle-Axe didn't deserve anything better.

Done! Now back to his comic. Screamin' Demon was just about to discover where the Master of the Macabre had hidden the treasure...

Horrid Henry felt a long fingernail poke into his shoulder. He looked up into Miss Battle-Axe's evil eye.

"...And why aren't you writing your story, Henry?" hissed Miss Battle-Axe.

Horrid Henry smiled.

"Because I finished it," said Henry.

"You...finished it?" said Miss Battle-Axe. She tugged on her ear. Perhaps it was time she had her earwax removed again.

"Yup," said Henry.

"Let me see," said Miss Battle-Axe, holding out her bony claw.

Tee-hee, thought Horrid Henry,

14

handing her the story. She doesn't
believe me. Wouldn't batty old Miss
Battle-Axe get a surprise.

"Hmmm," said Miss Battle-Axe
after she'd finished reading. "Hmmm.
Butterfly Fairies Paint the Rainbow.
Hmmm." She stared at Henry and tried
to smile but her mouth had trouble
turning up due to lack of practice.
"*Much* better than usual, Henry."

Henry stared. The men in white coats
would be coming to take Miss Battle-
Axe away any moment if she liked this
story better than his others.

"In fact…in fact…I want you to go now
to Miss Lovely's class and read it out loud
to the kindergartners. They'll love it."

What? NO!!!!!!!

Perfect Peter's class sat expectantly
on the carpet as Horrid Henry stood

before them, story in hand. Now everyone would think *he'd* written this stupid story. Moody Margaret would tease him until he was old and gray and toothless. But what could he do? He was trapped.

"*Putter fair pat the rainb…*" mumbled Horrid Henry.

"Speak up, Henry," said Miss Lovely. "Don't be shy. We're *so* looking forward to your story."

"*Butterfly Fairies Paint the Rainbow,*" hissed Horrid Henry.

Perfect Peter's jaw dropped. Too late Henry realized his mistake. Writing a story about butterfly fairies was bad enough. But he'd never hear the end of it if people found out he'd *copied* his younger brother's story. Though even Peter wouldn't be such a tattletale…would he?

Peter put his hand in the air.

"Miss Lovely, that's *my*—" began
Peter.

"Just kidding," said Horrid Henry
hastily. "My story is really called, uh,
Butterfly Fairies Fight the Giants."

He glanced down at his story,
changing words as he read:

"Once upon a time there lived two
hideous giants, King Hairy the Horrible
and Queen Gertrude the Gruesome.
Stamp and stomp, stomp and stamp
went the hideous giants every day.

"They liked stomping on fairies, especially the butterfly fairies who polished the rainbow every day.

"'One day the giants looked up at the sky. Whoopsy daisy! All the butterfly fairies had fallen off the rainbow.

"'Oh what fun,' cackled King Hairy the Horrible, squishing the blue butterfly fairy.

"'Yippee!' squealed Queen Gertrude the Gruesome, squashing the orange butterfly fairy.

"'Ha ha!' they both shrieked, stomping on the green butterfly fairy."

Perky Parveen looked shocked.

Spotless Sam began to sniff.

"'I'm going to roast those fairies for dinner,' said Queen Gertrude the Gruesome. 'Yum, yum!' she drooled as the delicious smell of cooked fairy

wafted through the castle kitchen.
Then the Queen picked up the fairy
bones and—"

Miss Lovely looked pale.

Oh no, what now, thought Horrid
Henry desperately. He'd reached Peter's
horrible fairy song.

"Tee-hee. Tra-la.
Tra-la tra-la
We are dainty little fairies
And we play and sing all day

Maybe you can come and join us
Then we'll paint the day away
Tee-hee hee hee
Tra-la-la-la."

Horrid Henry took a deep breath.

"King Hairy the Horrible and Queen Gertrude the Gruesome were so happy that they began to sing:

'Tee-hee. Ha ha. Ha ha ha ha.

We are big and ugly giants

And we belch and kill all day

Maybe we can come and find you

Then we'll squish your guts away

Tee-hee tee-hee

Ha ha ha ha,'"

bellowed Horrid Henry.

Perky Parveen began to cry.

"The fairwies got squished," sobbed Lisping Lily.

"I don't want the giants to eat the fairies," shrieked Tidy Ted.

"I'm scared," howled Helpful Hari.

"I want my mama," wept Needy Neil.

"Wah!" wailed the kindergartners.

Horrid Henry was thrilled. What a

reaction! Maybe I'll add a bit more, thought Horrid Henry. This is such a great story it's a shame to end it here.

"'Let's find some bunnies,' snarled the giants. 'I'm sure—'"

"Stop! Stop!" said Miss Lovely. She looked gray. "Better go back to your class," she whispered. What had Miss Battle-Axe been thinking?

Horrid Henry shook his head and closed the door on the screaming, howling class.

Wow. What a great story he'd written.

Maybe he should be an author when he grew up.

2

HORRID HENRY AND THE NUDIE FOODIE

"Children, I have some *thrilling* news," burbled Mrs. Oddbod.

Horrid Henry groaned. His idea of thrilling news and Mrs. Oddbod's idea of thrilling news were not the same. Thrilling news would be Mutant Max replacing Mrs. Oddbod as principal. Thrilling news would be Miss Battle-Axe being whisked off to ancient Rome to be a gladiator. Thrilling news would be Moody Margaret dumped in a swamp and Perfect Peter sent to prison.

Thrilling news wasn't new coat hooks and who was in the Good as Gold book.

But wait. What was Mrs. Oddbod saying? "Our school has been chosen to be a healthy-eating school. Our new healthy and nutritious school meals will be an example for schools everywhere."

Horrid Henry sat up. What? *Healthy* eating?

Oh no. Henry knew what grown-ups meant by healthy food. Celery. Beets. Eggplant towers. Anything that tasted yucky and looked revolting was bound to be

good for him. Anything
that tasted yummy was
bound to be bad. Henry
had plenty of healthy eating
at home. Was nowhere safe?

"And guess who's going to help
make our school a beacon
of healthy eating?"
babbled Mrs.
Oddbod. "Only
the world-famous
chef, Mr. Nudie Foodie."

Rude Ralph snorted. "Nudie," he
jeered.

Mr. Nudie Foodie?
thought Horrid Henry.
What kind of
stupid name was
that? Were there really
parents out there whose last
name was Foodie, who'd

decided that the perfect name for their son was Nudie?

"And here he is, in person," proclaimed Mrs. Oddbod.

The children clapped as a shaggy-haired man wearing a red-checked apron and a chef's hat bounced to the front of the auditorium.

"Starting today your school will be *the* place for delicious, nutritious food," he beamed. "I'm not nude, it's my food that's nude! My delicious, yummalicious grub is just plain scrummy."

Horrid Henry couldn't believe his ears. Just plain, delicious food? Why, that was *exactly* what Horrid Henry loved. Plain burgers. Plain pizzas with just cheese and nothing else. No sneaky flabby pieces of eggplant or grisly chunks of red pepper ruining the topping. Plain fries slathered in ketchup. Nothing funny. No strange green stuff. Three cheers to more burgers, more fries, and more pizza!

Horrid Henry could see it now. Obviously, *he'd* be asked to create the yummy new school menu of plain, delicious food.

Monday: chips, fries, ice cream, cake, burgers

Tuesday: burgers, fries, chips, chocolate

Wednesday: pizza, fries, chips, ice cream

Thursday: chocolate cake

Friday: burgers, pizza, fries, chips, cake, ice cream

(After all, it was the end of the week, and nice to celebrate.) Oh, and fizzywizz drinks every day and chocolate milk. There! A lovely, healthy, plain, nutritious, and delicious menu that everyone would love. Because, let's face it, at the moment school lunches *were* horrid. They only served burgers and fries once a week, thought Horrid

Henry indignantly. Well, he'd soon sort *that* out.

In fact, maybe *he* should be a famous chef when he got older. Chef Henry, the burger wizard. Happy Henry, hamburger hero. He would open a chain of famous restaurants, called,

   "Henry's! Where the eatin'

      can't be beaten!" Hmmm, well,

         he'd have time to improve the

      name while collecting his millions

every week from the restaurant tills as happy customers fought their way inside for the chance to chow down on one of Happy Henry's bun-tastic bu  everywhere would beg to eat there,

 safe in the knowledge that no vegetables

would ever contaminate their food.
Ahhh! Horrid Henry sighed.

Mr. Nudie Foodie was leaping up
and down with excitement. "And
you're all going to help me make the
delicious food that will be a joy to eat.
Remember, just like the words to
my hit song:

    It's not rude
    To be a dude
    Who loves nude food.
    Yee haw."

"Well, Nudie," said Mrs.
Oddbod. "Uhh, I mean, Mr.
Foodie…"

"Just call me Mr. Nudie Foodie," said
Mr. Nudie Foodie. "Now, who wants
to be a nudie foodie and join me in the
kitchen to make lunch today?"

"Me!" shouted Perfect Peter.
"Me!" shouted Clever Clare.

"I want to be a nudie foodie," said Jolly Josh.

"I want to be a nudie foodie," said Tidy Ted.

"I want to be a nudie foodie," yelled Greedy Graham. "I think."

"A healthy school is a happy school," said Mr. Nudie Foodie, beaming. "My motto is: only bad food boos, when you choose yummy food. And at lunchtime today, all your parents will be coming to the cafeteria to sample our scrumptious, yummalicious, fabulicious, and irresistible new food! Olé!"

Horrid Henry looked around the school kitchen. He'd never seen so many pots and pans and vats and cauldrons. So this was where the school glop was made. Well, not anymore. Would they be making giant whopper burgers in the huge frying pans? Or vats and vats of fries in the huge pots? Maybe they'd make pizzas in the gigantic ovens!

The Nudie Foodie stood before Henry's class. "This is so exciting," he said, bouncing up and down. "Everyone ready to make some delicious food?"

"Yes!" bellowed Henry's class.

"Right, then, let's get cooking," said Mr. Nudie Foodie.

Horrid Henry stood in front of a cutting board with Weepy William, Dizzy Dave, and Fiery Fiona. Fiery Fiona shoved Henry.

"Stop hogging the cutting board," she hissed.

Horrid Henry shoved her back,

 knocking the lumpy bag of ingredients onto the floor.

"Stop hogging it yourself," he hissed back.

"Wah!" wailed Weepy William. "Henry pushed me."

Wait. What was rolling all over the floor? It looked like...it couldn't be...

"Group 1, here's how to slice a yummy green pepper," beamed Mr. Nudie Foodie. "And Group 2, you're in charge of the tomatoes...Group 3, you make the broccoli salad. Group 4 will look after the mushrooms."

Green pepper? Tomatoes? Broccoli? Mushrooms? What was this muck?

"It's my yummy,

scrummy, super, secret, vege-tastic pasta sauce!" said Mr. Nudie Foodie.

What? What a dirty rotten trick. Where were the fries? Where were the burgers?

And then suddenly Horrid Henry understood Mr. Nudie Foodie's evil plan. He was going to sneak *vegetables* onto the school menu. Not just a single vegetable, but loads and loads and loads of vegetables. Enough evil vegetables to kill someone a hundred times over. Boy impaled by killer carrot.

Girl chokes
to death
on deadly
broccoli.
Boy gags on
toxic tomato.
Henry could
see the headlines
now. They'd find him dead in the
lunchroom, poisoned
by vegetables, his
limbs twisted
in agony…

Well, *no way*.
No way was this
foul fiend going to
trick Henry into
eating vegetables.

Everyone chopped
and stirred and mixed.
The evil brew hissed and bubbled.

Horrid Henry had never felt so cheated in his life.

Finally, the bell rang.

Mr. Nudie Foodie stood by the exit with an enormous black garbage bag.

"Before you leave, I want you to open your lunch boxes and dump all your junk food in here. No need for that stuff today."

"Huh?" said Rude Ralph.

"No!" wailed Greedy Graham.

"Yes!" said Mr. Nudie Foodie. "You'll thank me later."

Horrid Henry gasped in horror as everyone threw their yummy snacks into the bag as they filed out of the kitchen and ran out for recess. For once Henry was glad his mean, horrible parents never packed anything good in *his* lunch box.

Was there no end to this evil man's plots? thought Horrid Henry, stomping past Mr. Nudie Foodie into the hall. First, vegetable pasta sauce, then stealing everyone's snacks? What a waste. All those treats going straight into the garbage…

"Rescue us, Henry!" squealed the chocolate and chips trapped inside the garbage bag. "Help!"

Horrid Henry didn't need to be asked twice. He crept down the hall and darted back into the school kitchen.

Snacks, here I come, thought Horrid Henry.

The kitchen was empty. Huge vats of vegetable sauce sat ready to be poured onto pasta. What horrors would Mr. Nudie Foodie try to sneak on the menu tomorrow? And the next day? And the next? Just wait until the parents discovered the sauce was made of vegetables. They'd make the children eat this swill every day.

AAAAARRRRRGGGHHHHH.

And then suddenly Horrid Henry knew what he had to do. He  looked longingly at the enormous black garbage bag bulging with chips and chocolate and yummy snacks. Horrid Henry gritted his teeth. Sometimes you had to think ahead.  Sometimes you couldn't be distracted. Not even by doughnuts.

There wasn't a moment to lose. Any second a teacher or lunch lady could come in and foil him. He had to seize his chance to stop Mr. Nudie Foodie once and for all.

Grabbing whatever was nearest, Horrid Henry emptied a tin of salt into the first vat of sauce. Into the second went a tin of mustard powder. Into the third went a bottle of vinegar. Into the fourth and final one…

Henry looked at the gurgling, bubbling, poisonous, reeking, rancid, toxic sauce. Take that, Nudie Foodie, thought Horrid Henry, reaching for a tub of lard.

"What are you doing, Henry?" rasped a deadly voice.

Henry froze.

"Just looking for my lunch box," he said, pretending to search behind the cooking pots.

Miss Battle-Axe snarled, flashing her yellow brick teeth. She pointed to the door. Horrid Henry ran out.

Phew. What a lucky escape. Shame he hadn't completed his mission, but three vats out of four wasn't bad. Anyway, the fourth pot was sure to be disgusting, even without extra dollops of lard.

You are dead meat, Mr. Nudie Foodie, thought Horrid Henry.

"Parents, children, prepare yourselves for a taste sensation!" said Mr. Nudie

Foodie, ladling out pasta and sauce.

Lazy Linda's mother took a big forkful. "Mmm, doesn't this look yummy!" she said.

"It's about time this school served proper food," said Moody Margaret's mom, shoveling an enormous spoonful into her mouth.

"I couldn't agree more," said Tidy Ted's dad, scooping up pasta.

"BLECCCCHHHHH!" spluttered Margaret's mother, spitting it out all over

Aerobic Al's dad. Her face was purple. "That's disgusting! My Maggie Moo-Moo won't be touching a drop of that!"

"What are you trying to do, poison people?!" screamed Aerobic Al's Dad. His face was green.

"I'm not eating this muck!" shouted Clever Clare's mom. "And Clare certainly isn't."

"But…but…" gasped Mr. Nudie Foodie. "This sauce is my speciality, it's delicious, it's—" he took a mouthful.

"Uggghhhh," he said, spewing it all over Mrs. Oddbod. "It *is* disgusting."

Wow, thought Horrid Henry. Wow. Could the sauce really be *so* bad? He had to try it. Would he get the salty, the mustardy, the vinegary, or just the plain disgusting vegetably?

Henry picked up a tiny forkful of pasta, put it in his mouth and swallowed.

He was still breathing. He was still alive. Everyone at his table was slurping up the food and beaming. Everyone at the other tables was coughing and choking and spitting...

Horrid Henry took another teeny tiny taste.

The sauce was...delicious. It was much nicer than the regular glop they served at lunchtime with pasta. It was a million billion times nicer. And he had just...he had just...

"Is this some kind of joke?" gasped Mrs. Oddbod, gagging. "Mr. Nudie Foodie, you are toast! Leave here at once!"

Mr. Nudie Foodie slunk off.

"NOOOOO!" screamed Horrid Henry. "It's yummy! Don't go!"

Everyone stared at Horrid Henry.

"Weird," said Rude Ralph.

3

HORRID HENRY AND THE MAD PROFESSOR

Horrid Henry grabbed the top secret candy tin he kept hidden under his bed. It was jam-packed with all his favorites: Big Boppers. Nose Pickers. Dirt Balls. Hot Snot. Gooey Chewies. Scrunchy Munchies.

Yummy!!!

Mmmm boy! Horrid Henry's mouth watered as he prized off the lid. Which to have first? A Dirt Ball? Or a Gooey Chewy? Actually, he'd just scoff it all. It had been ages since he'd…

Huh?

Where were all his chocolates? Where were all his candy? Who'd swiped them? Had Margaret invaded his room? Had Peter sneaked in? How dare—Oh. Horrid Henry suddenly remembered. *He'd* eaten them all.

Rats.

Rats.

Triple rats.

Well, he'd just have to go and buy more. He was sure to have tons of pocket money left.

Chocolate, here I come, thought Horrid Henry, heaving his bones and dashing over to his skeleton bank.

He shook it. Then he shook it again.

There wasn't even a rattle.

How could he have *no* money and *no* candy? It was so unfair! Just last night Peter had been boasting about having $7.48 in *his* piggy bank. And loads of candy left over from Halloween. Horrid Henry scowled. Why did Peter *always* have money? Why did he, Henry, *never* have money?

Money was totally wasted on Peter. What was the point of Peter having money since he never spent it? Come to think of it, what was the point of Peter having candy since he never ate them?

There was a shuffling, scuttling noise, then Perfect Peter dribbled into Henry's bedroom carrying all his soft toys.

"Get out of my room, worm!" bellowed Horrid Henry, holding his nose. "You're stinking it up."

"I am not," said Peter.

"Are too, smelly pants."

"I do not have smelly pants," said Peter.

"Do too, woofy, poofy, stinky pants."

Peter opened his mouth, then closed it.

"Henry, will you play with me?" said Peter.

"No."

"Please?"

"No!"

"Pretty please?"

"No!!"

"But we could play school with all my cuddly toys," said Peter. "Or have a tea party with them…"

"For the last time, NOOOOOOO!" screamed Horrid Henry.

"You *never* play with me," said Perfect Peter.

"That's 'cause you're a toad-faced diaper wibble bibble," said Horrid Henry. "Now go away and leave me alone."

"Mom! Henry's calling me names again!" screamed Peter. "He called me wibble bibble."

"Henry! Don't be horrid!" shouted Mom.

"I'm not being horrid, Peter's annoying me!" yelled Henry.

"Henry's annoying *me!*" yelled Peter.

"Make him stop!" screamed Henry and Peter.

Mom ran into the room.

"Boys. If you can't play nicely then leave each other alone," said Mom.

"Henry won't play with me," wailed Peter. "He *never* plays with me."

"Henry! Why can't you play with your brother?" said Mom. "When I was little, Ruby and I played beautifully together all the time."

Horrid Henry scowled.

"Because he's a wormy worm," said Henry.

"Mom! Henry just called me a wormy worm," wailed Peter.

"Don't call your brother names," said Mom.

"Peter only wants to play stupid baby games," said Henry.

"I do not," said Peter.

"If you're not going to play together then you can do your chores," said Mom.

"I did mine," said Peter. "I fed Fluffy, cleaned out the litter tray, *and* tidied my room."

Mom beamed. "Peter, *you* are the best boy in the world."

Horrid Henry scowled. He'd been far too busy reading his comics to empty the wastepaper baskets and tidy his room. He stuck out his tongue at Peter behind Mom's back.

"Henry's making horrible faces at me," said Peter.

"Henry, *please* be nice for once and play with Peter," said Mom. She sighed and left the room.

Henry glared at Peter.

Peter glared at Henry.

Horrid Henry was about to push Peter out the door when suddenly he had a brilliant, spectacular idea. It was so brilliant and so spectacular that Horrid Henry couldn't believe he was still standing in his bedroom and hadn't blasted off into outer space trailing clouds of glory. Why had he never thought of this before? It was magnificent. It was genius. One day he would start Henry's Genius Shop, where people would pay a million dollars to buy his super fantastic ideas. But until then…

"Okay, Peter, I'll play with you," said Horrid Henry. He smiled sweetly.

Perfect Peter could hardly believe his ears.

"You'll...*play* with me?" said Perfect Peter.

"Sure," said Horrid Henry.

"What do you want to play?" asked Peter cautiously. The last time Peter

could remember Henry playing with
him they'd played Cannibals and
Dinner. Peter had had to be dinner…

"Let's play Robot and Mad
Professor," said Henry.

"Okay," said Perfect Peter. Wow.
That sounded a lot more exciting than
his usual favorite game—writing lists of
vegetables or having ladybug tea parties
with his stuffed toys. He'd probably

have to be the robot, and do what
Henry said, but it would be worth it to
play such a fun game.

"I'll be the robot," said Horrid Henry.

Peter's jaw dropped.

"Go on," said Henry. "You're the
mad professor. Tell me what to do."

Wow. Henry was even letting *him* be
the mad professor! Maybe
he'd been wrong about
Henry…maybe Henry
had been struck by
lightning and changed
into a nice brother…

"Robot," ordered Perfect
Peter. "March around the room."

Horrid Henry didn't budge.

"Robot!" said Peter. "I order you
to march."

"Pro—fes—sor! I—need—twenty-
five cents—to—move," said Henry in a

57

robotic voice. "Twenty-five cents. Twenty-five cents. Twenty-five cents."

"Twenty-five cents?" asked Peter.

"That's the rules of Robot and Mad Professor," said Henry, shrugging.

"Okay, Henry," said Peter, rummaging in his bank. He handed Henry twenty-five cents.

Yes! thought Horrid Henry.

Horrid Henry took a few stiff steps, then slowed down and stopped.

"More," said robotic Henry. "More. My batteries have run down. More."

Perfect Peter handed over another twenty-five cents.

Henry lurched around for a few
more steps, crashed into the wall and
collapsed on the floor.

"I need candy to get up," said the
robot. "Bring me candy. Systems
overload. Candy. Candy. Candy."

Perfect Peter dropped two pieces
of candy into Henry's hand. Henry
twitched his foot.

"More," said the robot. "Lots more."
Perfect Peter dropped four more

pieces of candy. Henry jerked up into a sitting position.

"I will now tell you my top secret— secret—secret—secret—" stuttered Horrid Henry. "Cross—my—palm— with—silver and sweets…" He held out his robot hands. Peter filled them.

Tee-hee.

"I want to be the robot now," said Peter.

"Okay, robot," said Henry. "Run upstairs and empty all the wastepaper baskets. Bet you can't do it in thirty seconds."

"Yes, I can," said Peter.

"Nah, you're too rusty and puny," said Horrid Henry.

"Am not," said Peter.

"Then prove it, robot," said Henry.

"But aren't you going to give me—" faltered Peter.

"MOVE!" bellowed Henry. "They don't call me the MAD professor for nothing!!!"

Playing Robot and Mad Professor was a bit less fun than Peter had anticipated. Somehow, his piggy bank was now empty and Henry's skeleton bank was full. And somehow most of Peter's Halloween candy was now in Henry's candy box.

Robot and Mad Professor was the most fun Henry had ever had playing with Peter. Now that he had all Peter's money and all Peter's sweets, could he trick Peter into doing all his chores as well?

"Let's play school," said Peter. That would be safe. There was no way Henry could trick him playing *that*...

"I've got a better idea," said Henry.

"Let's play Slaves and Masters. You're
the slave. I order you to…"

"No," interrupted Peter. "I don't
want to." Henry couldn't make him.

"Okay," said Henry. "We can play
school. You can be the classroom cleaner."

Oh! Peter loved being classroom cleaner.

"We're going to play Clean Up
the Classroom!" said Henry. "The
classroom is in here. So, get to work."

Peter looked around the great mess

of toys and dirty clothes and comics
and empty wrappers scattered all over
Henry's room.

"I thought we'd start by taking
attendance," said Peter.

"Nah," said Henry. "That's the baby
way to play school. You have to start
by tidying the classroom. You're the
classroom cleaner."

"What are you?" said Peter.

"The teacher, of course," said Henry.

"Can I be the teacher next?" said Peter.

"Sure," said Henry. "We'll swap after
you finish your job."

Henry lay on his bed and read his
comic and stuffed the rest of Peter's
candy into his mouth. Peter tidied.

Ah, this was the life.

"It's very quiet in here," said Mom,
popping her head around the door.
"What's going on?"

"Nothing," said Horrid Henry.

"Why is Peter tidying your room?" said Mom.

"'Cause he's the classroom cleaner," said Henry.

Perfect Peter burst into tears. "Henry took all my money and all my candy and made me do all his chores," he wailed.

"Henry!" shouted Mom. "You horrid boy!"

★ ★ ★

On the bad side, Mom made Henry give Peter back all his money. But on the good side, all his chores were done for the week. And he couldn't give Peter back his candy because he'd eaten it all.

Victory!

4

HORRID HENRY AND THE ZOMBIE VAMPIRE

"Isn't it exciting, Henry?" asked Perfect Peter, packing Bunnykins carefully in his Sammy the Snail overnight bag. "A museum sleepover! With a torch-lit trail! And work sheets! I can't think of anything more fun."

"I can," snarled Horrid Henry. Being trapped in a cave with Clever Clare reciting all the multiplication tables from one to a million. Watching *Cooking Cuties*. Even visiting Nurse Needle for one of her horrible injections. (Well, maybe not *that*.)

But *almost* anything would be better than being stuck overnight in Our Town Museum on a class sleepover. No TV. No computers. No comics. Why oh why did he have to do this? He wanted to sleep in his own comfy bed, not in a sleeping bag on the museum's cold, hard floor, surrounded by photos of old mayors and a few dusty exhibits.

AAARRRRGGGHH. Wasn't it bad enough he was bored all day in school without being bored all night too?

Worse, Peter's diaper baby class was coming too.

They'd probably have to be tucked in at seven o'clock, when they'd all start crying for their mamas. Ugghh. And then Miss Battle-Axe

snarling at them to finish thei
sheets, and Moody Margaret s
and Anxious Andrew whimper
he'd seen a ghost…

Well, no way was he going to that
boring old dump without some comics
to pass the time. He'd just bought the
latest *Screamin' Demon* with a big article
all about vampires and zombies. Yay!
He couldn't wait to read it.

Perfect Peter watched him stuff his
Mutant Max bag full
of comics.

"Henry, you know
we're not allowed to
bring comics to the
museum sleepover,"
said Perfect Peter.

"Shut up and mind
your own business,
toad," said Horrid Henry.

"Mom! Henry just called me a toad!" wailed Peter. "And he told me to shut up."

"Toady toady toady, toady toady toady," jeered Henry.

"Henry! Stop being horrid or no museum sleepover for you," yelled Mom.

Horrid Henry paused. Was it too late to be horrid enough to get banned from the sleepover? Why hadn't he thought of this before? Why, he could...

"Henry! Peter! We have to leave *now!*" yelled Dad.

Rats.

The children lined up in the museum's central hall clutching their sleeping bags as Miss Lovely and Miss Battle-Axe ticked off names on a big register.

"Go away, Susan," said Moody Margaret. "After what you did at my

house I'm going to sit with Gurinder.
So there."

"You're such a meanie, Margaret,"
said Sour Susan.

"Am not."

"Are too."

Susan scowled. Margaret was *always* so
mean. If only she could think of a way
to pay that old grouch back.

Margaret scowled. Susan was *always* so

annoying. If only she could think of a
way to pay that old fraidycat back.

Henry scowled. Why did he have to
be here? What he'd give for a magic
carpet to whisk him straight home to the
comfy black chair to watch *Terminator
Gladiator*. Could life get any worse?

"Henwy," came a little voice next
to him. "I love you Henwy. I want to
give you a big kiss."

Oh no, thought Horrid Henry. Oh no. It was Lisping Lily, New Nick's little sister. What was that foul fiend doing here?

"You keep away from me," said Horrid Henry, pushing and shoving his way through the children to escape her.

"Waaa!" wept Weepy William as Henry stepped on his foot.

"I want my mama," cried Needy Neil as Henry trampled on his sleeping bag.

"But I want to marry with you, Henwy," lisped Lily, trying to follow him.

"Henry! Stay still!" barked Miss Battle-Axe, glaring at him with her demon eyes.

"Hello, boys and girls, what an adventure we're going to have tonight," said the museum's guide, Earnest Ella, as she handed out pencils and work sheets.

Henry groaned. Boring! He hated work sheets.

"Did you know that our museum has a famous collection of balls of wool through the ages?" droned Earnest Ella. "And an old railway car? Oh yes, it's going to be an exciting sleepover night. We're even going on a torch-lit walk through the corridors."

Horrid Henry yawned and sneaked a peek at his comic book, which he'd hidden beneath his museum work sheet.

Watch out, demon fans!! To celebrate the release of this season's big blockbuster monster horror film, THE ZOMBIE VAMPIRES, study this checklist. Make sure there are no zombie vampires lurking in your neighborhood!!!!

Horrid Henry gasped as he read *How to Recognize a Vampire* and *How to*

Recognize a Zombie. Big, scary teeth? Big, googly eyes? Looks like the walking dead? Wow, that described Miss Battle-Axe perfectly. All they had to add was a big fat carrot nose and…

A dark shadow loomed over him.

"I'll take that," snapped Miss Battle-Axe, yanking the comic out of his hand. "*And* the rest."

Huh?

He'd been so careful. How had she spotted that comic under his work sheet? And how did she know about the secret stash in his bag? Horrid Henry looked around the hall. Aha! There was Peter, pretending not to look at him. How dare that wormy worm toad tell on him? Just for that…

"Come along, everyone, line up to collect your flashlights for our spooky walk," said Earnest Ella. "You wouldn't want to get left behind in the dark, would you?"

There was no time to lose. Horrid Henry slipped over to Peter's class and joined him in line with Tidy Ted and Goody-Goody Gordon.

"Hello, Peter," said Henry sweetly.

Peter looked at him nervously. Did Henry suspect *he'd* told on him? Henry didn't *look* angry.

"Shame my comic got confiscated," said Henry, "'cause it had a list of how to tell whether anyone you know is a zombie vampire."

"A zombie vampire?" asked Tidy Ted.

"Yup," said Henry.

"They're imaginary," said Goody-Goody Gordon.

"That's what they'd *like* you to believe," said Henry. "But I've discovered some."

"Where?" said Ted.

Horrid Henry looked around dramatically, then dropped his voice to a whisper.

"Two teachers at our school," hissed Henry.

"Two *teachers?*" said Peter.

"What?" said Ted.

"You heard me. Zombie vampires. Miss Battle-Axe *and* Miss Lovely."

"Miss *Lovely?*" gasped Peter.

"You're just making that up," said Gordon.

"It was all in *Screamin' Demon*," said Henry. "That's why Miss Battle-Axe grabbed my comic. To stop me from finding out the truth. Listen carefully."

Henry recited:

"How to recognize a vampire:

1. BIG HUGE SCARY TEETH.

"If Miss Battle-Axe's fangs were any bigger she would trip over them," said Horrid Henry.

Tidy Ted nodded. "She *does* have big pointy teeth."

"That doesn't prove anything," said Peter.

"2. DRINKS BLOOD."

Perfect Peter shook his head. "Drinks… blood?"

"*Obviously* they do, just not *in front* of people," said Horrid Henry. "That would give away their terrible secret."

"3. ONLY APPEARS AT NIGHT."

"But Henry," said Goody-Goody Gordon, "we see Miss Battle-Axe and Miss Lovely every day at school. They *can't* be vampires."

Henry sighed. "Have you been paying attention? I didn't say they were *vampires*, I said they were *zombie* vampires. Being half-zombie lets them walk around in daylight."

Perfect Peter and Goody-Goody Gordon looked at one another.

"Here's the total proof," Henry continued.

"How to recognize a zombie:

1. LOOKS DEAD.

"Does Miss Battle-Axe look dead? Definitely," said Horrid Henry. "I never saw a more dead-looking person."

"But Henry," said Peter. "She's alive."

Unfortunately, yes, thought Horrid Henry.

"Duh," he said. "Zombies always *seem* alive. Plus, zombies have scary, bulging eyes like Miss Battle-Axe," continued Henry. "And they feed on human flesh."

"Miss Lovely doesn't eat human flesh," said Peter. "She's a vegetarian."

"A likely story," said Henry.

"You're just trying to scare us," said Peter.

"Don't you see?" said Henry. "They're planning to pounce on us during the torch-lit trail."

"I don't believe you," said Peter.

Henry shrugged. "Fine. Don't believe me. Just don't say I didn't warn you when Miss Lovely lurches out of the dark and BITES you!" he shrieked.

"Be quiet, Henry," shouted Miss Battle-Axe. "William. Stop weeping.

There's nothing to be scared of. Linda!
Stand up. It's not bedtime yet. Bert!
Where's your flashlight?"

"I dunno," said Beefy Bert.

Miss Lovely walked over and smiled
at Peter.

"Looking forward to the torch-lit
walk?" she beamed.

Peter couldn't stop himself sneaking
a peek at her teeth. *Were* they big?
And sharp? Funny, he'd never noticed
before how pointy two of them were...
And was her face a bit...umm...pale?

No! Henry was just trying to trick
him. Well, he wasn't going to be fooled.

"Time to go exploring," said Earnest
Ella. "First stop on the torch-lit trail:
our brand-new exhibit, *Wonderful World
of Wool*. Then we'll be popping next
door down the *Passage to the Past* to visit
the old railway car and the Victorian

shop and a Neanderthal cave. Flashlights
on, everyone."

Sour Susan smiled to herself. She'd
just thought of the perfect revenge on
Margaret for teasing her for being such
a scaredy-cat.

Moody Margaret smiled to herself.
She'd just thought of the perfect
revenge on Susan for being so sour.

Ha ha, Margaret, thought Susan.
I'll get you tonight.

Ha ha, Susan, thought Margaret.
I'll get you tonight.

Ha ha, Peter, thought Henry. I'll get you tonight.

"Follow me," said Earnest Ella.

The children stampeded after her.

All except three.

When the coast was clear, Moody Margaret turned off her flashlight, darted into the pitch-black *Passage to the Past* hall, and hid in the Neanderthal cave behind the caveman. She'd leap out at Susan when she walked past. MWAHAHAHAHAHAHA! Wouldn't that old scaredy-cat get a fright.

Sour Susan turned off her flashlight and peeked down the *Passage to the Past* corridor. Empty. She tiptoed to the railway car and crept inside. Just wait till Margaret walked by…

Horrid Henry turned off his flashlight, crept down the *Passage to the Past*,

sneaked into the Victorian shop, and
hid behind the rocking chair.

Tee-hee. Just wait till Peter walked
past. He'd—

What was that?

Was it his imagination? Or did that
spinning wheel in the corner of the
shop…move?

CR—EEEK went the wheel.

It was so dark. But Henry didn't dare
switch on his flashlight.

Moody Margaret looked over from the Neanderthal cave at the Victorian shop. Was it her imagination or was that rocking chair rocking back and forth?

Sour Susan looked out from the railway car. Was it her imagination or was the caveman moving?

There was a strange, scuttling noise.

What was that? thought Susan.

You know, thought Henry, this museum *is* kind of creepy at night.

And then something grabbed onto his leg.

"AAAARRRRGGHHH!" screamed Horrid Henry.

★ ★ ★

Moody Margaret heard a blood-curdling scream. Scarcely daring to breathe, Margaret peeped over the caveman's shoulder…

Sour Susan heard a blood-curdling scream. Scarcely daring to breathe, Susan peeped out from the railway carriage…

"Henwy, I found you, Henwy," piped the creature clinging to his leg.

"Go away, Lily," hissed Henry. The horrible fiend was going to ruin everything.

"Will you marry me, Henwy?"

"No!" said Horrid Henry, trying to shake her off and brushing against the spinning wheel.

CR—EEEEK.

The spinning wheel spun.

What's that noise? thought Margaret, craning to see from behind the caveman.

"Henwy! I want to give you a big kiss," lisped Lily.

Horrid Henry shook his leg harder.

The spinning wheel tottered and fell over.

CRASH!

Margaret and Susan saw something lurch out of the Victorian shop and loom up in the darkness. A monstrous creature with four legs and waving arms...

"AAAARRRRGGHH!" screamed Susan.

"AAAARGGHHHHH!" shrieked Margaret.

"AAAARGGHHHHH!" shrieked
Henry.

The unearthly screams rang through the
museum. Peter, Ted, and Gordon froze.
  "You don't think—" gasped Gordon.
  "Not…" trembled Peter.
  "Zombie vampires?" whimpered Ted.
They clutched one another.
  "Everyone head back to the Central
Hall NOW!" shouted Earnest Ella.

★ ★ ★

In the cafeteria, Miss Lovely and Miss Battle-Axe were sneaking a short break to enjoy a lovely fried egg sandwich with lashings of ketchup.

Oh my weary bones, thought Miss Battle-Axe, as she sank her teeth into the huge sandwich. Peace at last.

AAARRGGHH! EEEEEKKK! HELLLP!

Miss Battle-Axe and Miss Lovely squeezed their sandwiches in shock as they heard the terrible screams.

SPLAT!

A stream of ketchup squirted Miss Lovely in the eye and dripped down her face onto her blouse.

SQUIRT!

A blob of ketchup splatted Miss Battle-Axe on the nose and dribbled down her chin onto her cardigan.

"Sorry, Boudicca," said Miss Lovely.

"Sorry, Lydia," said Miss Battle-Axe.

They raced into the dark central hall just as their classes ran back from the torch-lit walk. Fifty beams of light from fifty flashlights lit up the teachers' ketchup-covered faces and ketchup-stained clothes.

"AAAARRGGHHH!" screamed Perfect Peter.

"It's the zombie vampires!" howled Tidy Ted.

"Run for your lives!" yelped Goody-Goody Gordon.

"Wait!" shouted Miss Lovely. "Children, come back!"

"We won't eat you!" shouted Miss Battle-Axe.

"AAAARRRRGGHHHHHH!"

Acknowledgments

Jenny Gyertson has had her lovely story
Fairies Paint the Rainbow stolen
not once but twice: the least she deserves
is an acknowledgment.

My thanks also to Steven Butler
for telling me all about Theft
Number One…

The **HORRID HENRY** books
by Francesca Simon

Illustrated by Tony Ross
Each book contains four stories

HORRID HENRY
WAKES THE DEAD

Horrid Henry plots a brilliant plan for total TV control; schemes, bribes, and fights his way to become class president; battles with Peter over who gets the awesome purple dinosaur and who's stuck with the boring green one; and performs the greatest magic trick the world has ever seen at his school's talent contest.

HORRID HENRY ROCKS

Horrid Henry invades Perfect Peter's room; hunts for cookies in Moody Margaret's Secret Club tent, with frightening results; writes his biography—and Moody Margaret's; and plots to see the best band in the world (while his family wants to see the worst).

HORRID HENRY AND
THE ABOMINABLE SNOWMAN

Horrid Henry builds the biggest, meanest
monster snowman ever; writes his will (but
is more interested in what others should be
leaving him); starts his own makeover
business; and manages to thwart the Happy
Nappy for a chance
to meet his favorite
author in the
whole world.

HORRID HENRY'S UNDERPANTS

Horrid Henry discovers a genius way to write thank-you letters; negotiates over vegetables; competes with Perfect Peter over which of them is sickest; and finds himself wearing the wrong underpants—with dreadful consequences.

HORRID HENRY

Henry is dragged to dancing class against his will; vies with Moody Margaret to make the yuckiest Glop; goes camping; and tries to be good like Perfect Peter— but not for long.

About the Author

Photo: Francesco Guidicini

Francesca Simon spent her childhood on the beach in California and then went to Yale and Oxford Universities to study medieval history and literature. She now lives in London with her family. She has written over forty-five books and won the Children's Book of the Year in 2008 at the Galaxy British Book Awards for *Horrid Henry and the Abominable Snowman.*